THE LONG, HOT RECESS

by Erica Pass

illustrated by Barry Goldberg

SCHOLASTIC INC.

New York Toronto London Auckland Sydney
Mexico City New Delhi Hong Kong Buenos Aires

Butch Hartman (signature)

Based on the TV series *The Fairly OddParents*® created by Butch Hartman as seen on Nickelodeon®

No part of this publication may be reproduced in whole or in part, or stored in a retrieval system, or transmitted in any form or by any means, electronic, mechanical, photocopying, recording, or otherwise, without written permission of the publisher. For information regarding permission, write to Simon Spotlight, Simon & Schuster Children's Publishing Division, 1230 Avenue of the Americas, New York, NY 10020.

ISBN 0-439-66671-6

Copyright © 2004 by Viacom International Inc. All rights reserved. NICKELODEON, The Fairly OddParents, and all related titles, logos, and characters are trademarks of Viacom International Inc. Published by Scholastic Inc., 557 Broadway, New York, NY 10012, by arrangement with Simon Spotlight, Simon & Schuster Children's Publishing Division. SCHOLASTIC and associated logos are trademarks and/or registered trademarks of Scholastic Inc.

12 11 10 9 8 7 6 5 4 3 2 1   4 5 6 7 8 9/0

Printed in the U.S.A.

First Scholastic printing, November 2004

Timmy Turner and his friends were at school. Even though it was recess, they weren't having much fun. It had been raining for two weeks straight.

"I'm bored," Timmy said.

"Me too," his friend Chester added.

"Even *I'm* bored," said their friend A.J., "and I never get bored when I'm doing complex math problems in my head."

After school the guys went to Timmy's house to play the new Crash Nebula video game.

"I'm still bored," Timmy said after an hour.

"Me too," Chester added.

"Even *I'm* bored, and I just got three extra lives," said A.J. "Eat my bored dust!"

Timmy decided he *really* needed to talk to his fairy godparents. He stepped behind the TV set and pulled the cord out of the wall. *ZAP!*—Crash Nebula was gone.

"Hey!" A.J. shouted. "Just when I was about to get crowned king of planet Chromalon!"

"Oh well, better luck next time!" Timmy said. "Here's an umbrella for the rain. See ya!"

Timmy ran up the stairs to his room to find Cosmo and Wanda.

"Hi, guys," said Timmy. "Listen, school's *boring*!"

"Really?" said Wanda. "But it's so educational!"

"And the rain," Timmy continued. "It's *boring*."

"Really? But it's so wet!" said Cosmo.

"I don't care!" Timmy said. "I'm bored! I'm tired of school and I'm tired of the rain! I'm even getting tired of video games!"

"Well I'm getting tired of Wanda, but don't tell her that!" Cosmo said.

"I have an idea," continued Timmy, "for a super-duper *double* wish!"

Cosmo and Wanda flipped through the pages of Da Rules. "Well, look at that. You're allowed one super-duper double wish per year."

"Cool!" Timmy said. He rubbed his hands together. "I wish for it to be sunny all the time! And . . . I wish it was summer vacation every day!"

And with that—POOF!—Dimmsdale was drenched in sunlight. Kids poured out of their homes and onto the sidewalks. They were everywhere!

"Cool!" Timmy yelled. "It's just like a summer morning!" He ran downstairs.

"Where are you going, Timmy?" asked Mrs. Turner.

"You should eat some cereal before you catch the school bus,"
Mr. Turner said.

"But look, guys!" Timmy shouted as he clicked the TV on.

"It's summer vacation in Dimmsdale—all the time. And boy is it sunny!
This is Chet Ubetcha, signing off."

"See? No school," Timmy said as he ran outside.

"Hey, guys!" Timmy pushed through the crowd of kids mobbing the ice-cream truck to find Chester and A.J. "No more rain, no more books, no more Crocker's dirty looks."

"I scream, you scream, we all scream for . . . no school!" Chester cried.

Timmy and his friends stayed outside for hours eating ice cream and playing.

"Woo hoo! Let's hit the sprinkler, Wanda!" Cosmo yelled.

"Sweetie, don't forget to wear your sunscreen," Wanda said. "You know how you burn!"

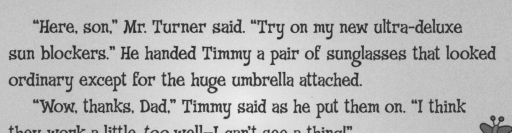

"Here, son," Mr. Turner said. "Try on my new ultra-deluxe sun blockers." He handed Timmy a pair of sunglasses that looked ordinary except for the huge umbrella attached.

"Wow, thanks, Dad," Timmy said as he put them on. "I think they work a little *too* well—I can't see a thing!"

The next day Timmy had ice cream for breakfast again and played with his friends all day long.

DAY 1

DAY 4

By the twelfth day of Dimmsdale's permanent summer vacation Timmy was still into the routine. Not everyone was quite as excited. The sun was so strong that no one could escape the bright sunlight long enough to fall asleep.

Even Cosmo and Wanda weren't their usual perky selves.

"Waaaahh," Cosmo cried. His face was bright red with sunburn. "It hurts! I want my mommy! And my mommy's sunblock."

Timmy pointed at Wanda, whose eyes were closed. "Hey, Wanda, are you asleep?" Timmy asked.

Wanda struggled to open her eyelids. "My eyes feel cracked as a broken eggshell, but I can't fall asleep because it's still too bright out. If only *I* could wish this sun to stop!" Wanda said drowsily.

Timmy went outside where
Chester and A.J. sat slumped against each
other. "Ready for another fun-filled, sun-filled day?"
Timmy asked.

"I'm tired of the sun," said Chester.

"Let's go to the arcade," A.J. said. "It's one of the only places
that isn't sunny."

"But I thought the whole point was to be outside since it
is sunny!" Timmy shouted after them. "Um . . . guys?"

"Hey, Turner!" called a familiar voice behind him.

Timmy cringed. *Vicky.*

"I'm baby-sitting while your parents go to the new all-day/all-night tennis courts," Vicky said. "You want to be out in the sun? *I'll* keep you out in the sun. Now hose down the lawn!" She stomped into the house.

"This stinks!" Timmy said. "The sun has made everyone too tired to play. I miss Wanda. I miss Crash Nebula. I even miss . . . the rain!"

"But isn't this what you wanted?" asked Cosmo, appearing by Timmy's side.

"It seemed a lot more fun in my head," Timmy said, sighing.

Just then Timmy got an idea. He ran into the house and grabbed his dad's sunglasses.

"Hey, twerp!" Vicky screeched. "Are you done with the lawn yet? I need you to slather sunscreen on my dear dog, Doidle."

"Right!" Timmy said over his shoulder. "That's next on my list of things that I can't wait to do for you."

In his bedroom Timmy placed the sunglasses on his windowsill. His room went dark.

"Okay, Wanda, you can get some sleep now." Timmy said, "and when you wake up, we can get back to exercising our brains."

The next morning Wanda was more like herself. Even Cosmo's sunburn had faded to a nice shade of pink.

"I guess you guys were right," Timmy said. "It's better to have day and night, sun and rain, school and vacation."

So Timmy wished for things to be back the way they were—rain, school, and all. But before he did, he made one last promise to his godparents.

"I promise you guys that I'll never ever say 'I'm bored' again!"

"Sure you won't, Timmy," said Cosmo and Wanda. "Sure you won't."